Jim and the Pirates

by

ELEANOR FARJEON

Illustrated by
JULIETTE PALMER

KAYE & WARD LTD
194–200 Bishopsgate
London EC2

First published in volume form by
KAYE & WARD LIMITED
194–200 Bishopsgate, London EC2
1967

Reprinted by
KAYE & WARD LIMITED
194–200 Bishopsgate, London EC2
1969

Phototypeset by Keyspools Ltd,
Golborne, Lancashire

Printed in England by
C. Tinling & Co. Ltd,
Liverpool, London and Prescot

Jim and the Pirates

'Jim,' said Derry, 'when you were a sailor were you a Pirate?'

Jim took his empty pipe out of his mouth, looked into it, knocked it out on the breakwater, looked into it again, pulled out a knife, and a plug of twist, and began, slowly and carefully, to stuff the bowl of his pipe with black tobacco. He did not seem to hear Derry's question, or to see the ring of small attentive faces that hung upon

his answer. The owners of the faces were squatting on a /shelving bank of /shingle against the breakwater. Most of them were in bathing-dresses, for the month was August and the hour was noon. They had already bathed once, and several of them had bathed twice, and a good many of them intended to bathe three times. What did you come to the seaside *for*? It was a splendid thing to be able to say, when you got home, 'On August the nineteenth I bathed five times, and paddled twice.'

Derry had not told his new summer-holiday friend, /Quentin, that he hoped to beat him at bathing before they went home, and /Quentin hadn't let on to Derry that he knew Derry was jolly well trying to, and he, Quentin, was jolly well not going to let him if *he* could help it. Every day Quentin and Derry got down to the sands a bit earlier than the day before, in order to be able to work in an extra bathe, carelessly as though it wasn't exactly happening; but each guessed what the other was about though of course they were firm friends. Hadn't they got to know each other from morning to night for a fortnight and three days and sworn blood-brothership when Derry cut his shin on a broken bottle while paddling? It seemed a pity not to take advantage of so much good blood, and, as Derry said generously, 'You needn't cut *your* self, Quen, my blood'll do for both.'

After all, it was up to him to do something, he considered, for a chap with the name of Quentin da Costa; just having a blood-brother with a name like that was valuable in itself. It wasn't every boy in Derry's school who would be able to come back next term remarking, 'Well, my friend Quentin da Costa says . . .' Quentin da Costa would only be able to remark, 'Well my friend Derry Vane says . . .' And, blood-brothers though they were Derry didn't think Quentin would remark it.

And then, Jim arrived! Jim-at-the-Corner, the old sailor who sat at Derry's very street-corner in London, who had been everywhere and done everything (he had even been to places that nobody else ever heard of, and done things nobody else ever dreamed of). It was years and years since Jim had seen the sea, and Derry's father himself had arranged for the old salt to spend a fortnight at Selsey where Derry was summer-holidaying and on Jim's birthday Derry and Mr. Vane had driven to town in the motor-car, and fetched Jim away as a surprise. And it *was* a surprise—such a surprise that it seemed to have taken Jim's breath away; for when Derry called to see him at the fisherman's cottage where he was being lodged, Jim had none of the tales handy that he told so freely when he sat on his orange-box at the corner of the London street. So Derry gave him a day to get his breath in, and on the second morning he pointed Jim out to Quentin as they ran out of the sea after their second bathe. Here was something he could do for Quentin at last! It wasn't every chap who had a friend like Jim to introduce to a chap.

He pointed a wet brown finger at the old sailor, who sat smoking by the breakwater, staring at the sea. 'Look!' said Derry.

'What?' asked Quentin.

'You see that man over there?'

'Well, I'm not exactly blind, am I?'

Derry doubled up with mirth. It was this kind of thing that made Quentin such a splendid person to have for a friend. When Derry had done laughing, Quentin said, 'What about the blighter?'

'I know him,' said Derry. 'He's a sailor. He's not like the sailors here who fish and that. He's awfully old, and he ran away to sea to be a cabin-boy, and the ship was called the *Rockinghorse*, and the Captain was Cap'n Potts, and they had tremendous adventures, shipwrecks and ice-bergs and things. He's seen the Sea-Serpent.'

'Go on!' said Quentin. But he looked impressed, and so did Effie and Janet McTavish, and the three Brownings, who had stopped to listen on their way back to the huts.

'What's his name?' asked Quentin.

'Jim,' said Derry.

'Has he ever been a Pirate?' asked Quentin.

'Oh, I expect so,' said Derry. 'He's been almost everything.'

'Don't you *know* if he's been a Pirate?' asked Quentin.

'Well, he hasn't told me *all* his tales yet,' said Derry. 'Let's go and ask him.'

The children trailed over the beach after Derry and Quentin, and as they drew nearer Janet McTavish said, 'He

15

must be a Pirate, he's got ear-rings.'

'They came off the tip of the Sea-Serpent's tail,' said Derry, and waved his hand to him, who saluted and called, 'Hello, little 'un. Had a nice dip?'

'Yes, thank you,' said Derry. 'This is my friend Quentin da Costa, Jim, and these two are Effie and Janet McTavish, and these three are Evelyn and Valentine and Marion Browning. They're boys, though.'

'That's all right,' said Jim nodding to the group of children, who settled round him expectantly.

It was then that Derry, leaning his elbows on Jim's knee (though he didn't really *mean* to show off), asked, 'When you were a sailor were you a Pirate?'

16

And it was then that Jim took his pipe out of his mouth and began the slow process of knocking it out and

filling it again. Derry always understood (Jim had given him to understand it very early in their acquaintance) that this important ceremony must not be interrupted on any account whatever.

But Quentin did not know this, and as Jim pulled his pouch out of his pocket, he backed up Derry's question with another. 'And did you ever find a Treasure on an island?'

Jim paused, with his finger in the pipe-bowl. 'Da Costa, is that your name?' he inquired.

Quentin nodded, pleased that Jim had remembered it.

'Then look you here, young da Costa,' said Jim. 'You'd ought to know more of the ways of the sea than to speak to the man at the plug.'

'I say,' said Quentin, getting rather red. 'Why not?'

'You mustn't disturb the man what's filling his pipe,' explained Jim, 'no more than the man what's steering the ship. For why? It's fatal to the attention. Talk to the man at the wheel, and it may be a good ship spoiled. Talk to the man at the plug, and it may be a good pipe spoiled. As a ship must sail just *so*, and a pipe must draw just *so*. It depends on the wind in both cases.'

'I see,' said Quentin humbly. 'I'm awfully sorry.'

'That's all right,' said Jim. 'You'll know next time.' He went on cutting the plug and filling his pipe, while the children watched him, scarcely daring to breathe. At last the pipe was stuffed, a match had been found and struck, and Jim had taken the first three meditative pulls. To the relief of everybody a cloud of smoke issued from his mouth. 'Now then.' Jim removed the pipe for an instant. 'What was it you both of you wanted to know?'

'I wanted to know if you'd ever been a Pirate, Jim,' said Derry.

'And I wanted to know if you'd ever found a Treasure on an island,' said said Quentin. 'And I'd awfully like to know too, if you don't mind, why you thought I ought to know the ways of the sea because of my name.'

'Now we're coming to it,' said Jim. 'When Derry here mentioned that name of yours, I began to wonder a bit.'

'I say! What?' exclaimed Quentin. For the last three minutes he had been just a little bit like a balloon with the air running out; but at Jim's remark the air seemed to run in again.

'I wondered,' said Jim, puffing thoughtfully, 'If you could be by any accident a great-grandson, or great-great-grandson maybe, of Rico da Costa, the notorious Pirate.'

'I *say*!' The air-balloon was full to bursting-point.

'Just you keep quiet,' said Jim, 'and *I'll* do the saying.'

Have I ever been a Pirate? No, I have *not*. The Union Jack was good enough for me. But that's not to say I never sailed with a Pirate, for you never knew your luck on the High Seas. And Treasure? My word, Treasure! I've took Treasure, and I've lost Treasure; I've buried Treasure, and I've dug it up. I've looked for it and not found it, and found it when I wasn't looking for it. Treasure? I should say so! And the Treasure I remember more than any other was that I was forced to go looking for with Rico da Costa, the most notorious Pirate on the Spanish Main, when he captured the good ship *Rockinghorse* with all hands aboard.

We'd sailed from Bristol City, bound

for Lima, with a cargo of soda-water siphons. They were wanted bad in Lima, where the lime-juice was plentiful, and the water not fit to drink with it. Those South American rivers are full of pythons, and they don't do the water no good. It brings the Limen out in bumps. Pythonitis they call it, and if you scratch it's fatal. They always did

scratch, and died off like flies. So one voyage when we were drinking lime-juice-cordial neat with the Head Liman, Cap'n Potts tossed off his third pint, and put down his tankard, and said, 'You can't go on like this.'

'We have to,' said the Head Liman. 'Or die of thirst. Or Pythonitis.'

'No have-to about it,' says Cap'n Potts. 'The cure for Pythons is syphons. I'll get you some.'

'You shall have their weight in rubies if you do,' said the Head Liman.

'Done!' said Cap'n Potts. He had a second cousin who ran a soda-water syphon factory in Somerset, and that's how our crew for the return trip came to be picked up in Bristol City.

Of course, Cap'n Potts had the best part of his crew already. He stuck to us, and we stuck to him. There never was a deserter from the *Rockinghorse*, but now and then one of the crew fell out of step for a voyage, for one reason or another. It happened this time that we were fitting out the ship for her trip during the spring-cleaning season, and most of the crew were lending their missuses a hand at home in the meantime. The night before we sailed two of 'em came aboard and said to Cap'n Potts, 'Very sorry Cap'n, but we can't come along this voyage.'

'Can't come along?' said Cap'n Potts. 'You've got to come along. D'ye suppose I can sail to Lima two hands short?'

'I don't see what's to be done about it,' said one of the chaps.

'Our missuses aren't through yet, and I've promised to whitewash the kitchen tomorrow, and Jack here promised his wife he'd stain the parlour surround.'

'Well, that is a nuisance,' said Cap'n Potts. There was nothing for it but to let the men go, and they went. And the Cap'n sent for me and told me the news and said, 'Come along o' me, Jim, and see what we can find in Bristol to take the lubbers' places. But I'll smash my Toby-Jug,' said he, 'if I take another married man along, if he were the best seaman in Britain. Bachelors and widowers, Jim, that's what we're after.'

So we went ashore to look for bachelors and widowers.

Well, we found seamen who were
married men with wives; and bachelors
and widowers who weren't seamen.
It's a peculiar thing how married
sailors are. In the end we found but
two who answered to the requirements.
One was a long thin pale-faced fellow,
who looked as though he couldn't say
Boo to a goose. The other was a thick,

dark, greasy ruffian, who looked as though he'd swallowed both goose and gander. We didn't fancy the looks of either of 'em, but Cap'n Potts put to each his two main questions.

'Are you a sailor?' he asked, sharp and short, so as to startle the truth out of 'em.

And they both said yes, they were.

'Are you a lawful married man?' he popped out next.

And they both said no, they weren't.

Then Cap'n Potts drew me aside and said, 'What do you think, Jim?'

'I think,' I said, 'it's a pity they ain't found some good woman to marry 'em. But you can't be surprised at it, and they being the only two single sailors

left in Bristol, you'll have to take 'em, or smash your Toby-Jug.'

'I don't want to do that,' said Cap'n Potts. 'It was a legacy from my grand-aunt. She filled and emptied it twenty times a day until she died. A grand-aunt, Jim. Pity she died so young.'

'How old?' I asked.

'I don't remember,' said Cap'n Potts. 'I wasn't born at the time. By all accounts she died the second day after she bought the Toby.' Then he turned to the fair and sickly man and the dark and stout one. 'Sign on, my lads,' he said, 'or make your mark.'

The fair one signed, and the dark one made his mark. Their names were Simon Sugar and Orinoco. I leave you to guess for yourselves which man was which. The crew being complete, we sailed next day, and for the first time in my recollection we sailed with an uncomfortable feeling. We didn't like Orinoco, and we couldn't love Simon Sugar. We were sorry for the latter, because of a nasty cough he'd been considerate enough to keep under during the signing on. Once aboard, he coughed fit to shake the *Rockinghorse* out of her course. Cap'n Potts went in and rubbed him night and morning till the camphorated oil gave out, but it didn't do him any good, though he was grateful. He was the most pathetic sailor I ever sailed with; and he hated Orinoco like poison. Orinoco used to mimic his cough when Cap'n Potts was out of hearing. If he'd done it in hearing he would have been sent to Coventry.

It looked as though the *Rockinghorse* was going to make a tame trip; nothing out of the common happened to us till we got within a day or so of Lima. Then one morning, as I was giving Simon Sugar his eleven o'clock gruel he sits up in bed, looks through the porthole at the sea-water, and says in an anxious sort of voice, 'Whereabouts are we, mate?'

'Two days off Lima,' I told him.

'Lima!' cried Simon, going as white as granulated. 'And I thought we were bound for Lyme Regis. If I'd ha' known, I'd never ha' signed on.'

'You ought to have asked then,' I said, 'or looked.'

'If we'd been bound for Lyme,' I observed, 'we'd ha' been there and back forty times by now, starting from Bristol as we did.'

'It's not the starting-point that counts,' said Simon Sugar, 'it's which way round you go. Anyways, a man with a cough like mine don't take no heed of time. Jim,' he says, 'go to the Captain and say I want to see him.'

I went to the bridge and told the Cap'n; and Cap'n Potts said, 'I've thought for weeks that Sugar had something on his mind, Jim, for it's certain he's got something on his chest.'

'Meaning his cough?' I inquired.

'It's before you come to his cough,' said Cap'n Potts, 'it's a parchment map he keeps there, taking it off before I rub the oil in, and putting it back when I've done.'

'P'raps he keeps it there for consolation,' I suggested.

'Well, since he's sent for me,' said Cap'n Potts, 'I'll have you there as a witness. Only somebody must mind the bridge while I'm away.'

He cast his eye about and every man jack of the crew seemed to be doing something he couldn't be took off doing, except Orinoco and the Bosun.

'Bosun's your man,' I said.

'I wish it might be so,' said Cap'n

Potts, 'but it's his birthday. No, there's nothing for it but Orinoco.' And he gave Orinoco a hail.

'It's only for five minutes, after all,' I said, as Orinoco came up, showing his teeth in the sort of smile that reminded me of crocodiles.

'Just keep an eye on the bridge while I'm gone,' said Cap'n Potts. 'I shan't be long.'

'Take your time, Cap'n,' says Orinoco, affably.

Then I and the Captain went below to Simon Sugar; and as soon as we got inside the cabin he declares, 'Cap'n Potts, I want to go back.'

'Back where?' asked Cap'n Potts.

'Bristol City,' said Sugar. 'Turn the

Rockinghorse round and take me home.'

'Now, Simon, be reasonable,' said Cap'n Potts soothingly. 'I can't do that without letting the Limen down. What's your objection to Lima?'

'It isn't Lima,' said Simon, 'it's the latitude. I never meant to sail these latitudes again.'

But before Simon could tell why not, the *Rockinghorse* got a bump. Next moment the air was full of shouts and the sound of grappling-irons. The shouts might have meant anything from Land-ahoy to waterspouts; but grappling-irons on the High Seas mean one thing, and one thing only. Pirates.

Pirates it was. A moment later Cookie knocked at the door and said,

'Excuse me, Cap'n, if you're engaged, but we've just been captured.'

'I thought as much,' said Cap'n Potts. 'Who's responsible?'

'Rico da Costa,' said Cookie, 'the most notorious Pirate on the High Seas.'

'Who says so?' asks Cap'n Potts.

'He does,' says Cookie. 'And he says, will you be so good as to come on deck, along of anybody else as may be below.'

'Come along, Jim,' says Cap'n Potts, 'and you too, Sugar.'

'I can't get up today,' said Simon Sugar, 'my cough's too bad. It'd be the death of me.'

'All right,' said Cap'n Potts, 'I'll tell him.' So he and I and Cookie went up aloft, and I knew by the set of the Captain's mouth that there was dirty weather ahead.

The sight on board the *Rockinghorse* was enough to make you pipe your eye. The deck was black with Pirates, and we was hitched up to the side of as foul a looking craft as ever I want to set eyes on. The *Marrowbone*, that was the name on her, and her figure-head was a buccaneer gnawing a monstrous bone like a mouth-organ. But dirt! You never saw so much dirt on a ship in your born days! Enough to make an able-bodied seaman sick, who kept a ship like a pin, as we did the *Rockinghorse*.

But we hadn't much time to take these details in because we found ourselves confronted by Rico da Costa himself; he was seven foot high, and his mouth was so full of teeth that he couldn't shut it.

'Cap'n Potts,' he barked as soon as we appeared.

'And no other,' said the Cap'n.

'You're my prisoner,' said Rico.

'So I understand,' said Cap'n Potts, rather stiffly.

'Stay put,' roared Rico, 'till I've done questioning you; and you'—he turned to me, 'go over there.'

He pointed aft, where all the crew was gathered except the Bosun who was sitting thinking on a bale of rope.

'Ain't Bosun coming too?' I asked.

'I told him to,' said Rico, 'but he

says it's his birthday, and he's off duty.'

'It *is* my birthday,' says Bosun looking up, 'and I wish you would not interrupt my thoughts. I am a triplet, and I spend every birthday thinking of my brothers, and they do the same by me. It's a family fixture.'

'Get on with it then,' says Rico, 'but if I find you're deceiving me, I'll slice you into eight!'

'My sailors speak the truth,' said Cap'n Potts proudly. 'I never shipped but one I couldn't trust. That one there!' and he turned like a flash of lightning on Orinoco, who was standing all this while in Rico's shadow.

Orinoco swaggered a little and tried to brazen it out. 'What, me, Cap'n?' he

said.

'Yes you,' said Cap'n Potts. 'You were a Pirate all the while! You signed on for this purpose! You took advantage of your control of the bridge to run the *Rockinghorse* into Rico's grapnel.'

'Right three times!' retorted Rico da Costa. 'And now we know where we are. So, Cap'n, we'll come down to brass tacks. What's your cargo?'

'Soda-water,' said Cap'n Potts.

'Drat it!' cursed Rico. 'Are you certain sure?'

'Dead certain,' said Cap'n Potts; 'you'll find nothing but syphons in the hold, Mr. Pirate.'

'Then all I can say is, it's a blind!' said Rico. 'Whoever heard of a Prize Ship sailing the Spanish Main with syphons of soda? Ah Cap'n, you're a clever one, you are! It's Treasure you're after, and you've loaded up with soda-water to discourage me. Now then! What buried Treasure do you know of? What island are you bound for? Out with it!'

'Stuffy-nonsense,' said Cap'n Potts.

'I'll show you if it's stuffy-nonsense,' bellowed Rico. 'If you don't produce your map before I count three, I'll brain you with your own anchor.' And he picked up the anchor with one hand, as easy as if it was a toothpick, and cried:

'ONE!'

Cap'n Potts stood firm, every inch a man.

'TWO!' cried Rico da Costa.

Still Cap'n Potts didn't flinch.

Then Rico da Costa opened his jaws to shout 'THREE!' and swung the anchor above his ugly head; but before the sound got past his teeth, Simon Sugar's pale face appeared in the hatchway, and he held up his finger at

Rico, while he got over a fit of coughing.

Rico da Costa put down the anchor and stared at him. 'Hello! he said, 'Who are you? That's a nasty cough you've got.'

As soon as he could speak, Simon agreed. 'It is. A very nasty cough. I want to go home.'

'Where's that?' asked Rico da Costa.

'Bristol City. Now listen to me,' said Simon Sugar gently. 'You can see for yourself how it is with me. Not fit to lift my finger to a fly. Weak as a new-born babe. You've no call to fear me.'

'I hadn't thought of doing so,' said Rico da Costa.

'Very well, then. By rights I oughtn't to be out of my bunk; but when I heard

you threaten Cap'n Potts it wasn't in me to think of myself. That man has rubbed me night and morning back and front. It's up to me to do what little I can for him. Now listen to me,' said Simon Sugar again. 'Cap'n Potts has told you the level truth; the object of this voyage is soda-water, and nothing but. Only, though *he* doesn't know it, there *is* a map of an island on this ship, where a Treasure is to be found; and only I can tell you where it is.'

'I'll make you tell me at the point of the cutlass,' blustered Rico, flourishing his cutlass.

'There's no call,' said Simon Sugar, 'for you to point your cutlass *or* to laugh in that nasty little way. I'm going to tell you without any making. All I want is to go home after I've told.'

'How'll we manage that?' asked Rico da Costa.

'Easy,' said Simon Sugar. 'Put me and Bosun into the jolly-boat. He'll row me to Lima where we'll take ship for England. *I'm* no good to you and *he's* no good to you, so you might as well let us go.'

'Oh I dare say,' jeered Rico, 'and let you tell the Limen all about me.'

'I'll tell them nothing,' said Simon Sugar. 'I only want to be quit of you. As for Bosun, he isn't, in a manner of speaking, here at all.'

'I am not,' said the Bosun. 'I'm in Margate, catching shrimps with Alfie and Alf. I don't know who you are and I don't want to know. Leave me be.'

Rico da Costa let the Bosun be and turned his attention again to Simon Sugar. 'There's something in what you say,' he remarked, 'and I'm inclined to agree. Only first I want to know about this Treasure. Is it a big one?'

'Enormous,' said Simon Sugar.

'Why did you leave it on the island?' asked Rico.

'It was more than I could bear,' said Simon Sugar. 'All I thought of was getting away with a whole skin. One night an empty boat was tossed up on the shore. It was my first and only chance of escape. My Treasure would have sunk the boat; so I just went.

I rowed and rowed until I got to Lima; and when I got there I made a chart of the latitude and longitude of the island, so that I should never forget where my Treasure was.'

'How came you to be on the island?' asked Rico da Costa.

'I'd been marooned by the captain of my ship,' said Simon.

'What for?' asked Rico.

'I wasn't popular with the crew,' said Simon.

'And what about this Treasure on the island?' asked Rico. 'How many men would it make rich for life?'

'It would do for any fifty men,' said Simon.

The eyes of the Pirates shone with greed at his words. There were exactly fifty of them, you see.

'Well, where's that map?' asked Rico da Costa.

'Here,' said Simon Sugar. He laid his hand on his chest. Rico da Costa made a movement towards him; but Cap'n Potts held up his hand and checked him.

'Rico,' he said, 'the map is this miserable man's sole chest-protector. There's two yards of Welsh flannel in my cabin; you'll find it in the deep end of my writing-desk.'

'What do you keep it there for?' asked the Pirate.

'I have to keep it somewhere,' said Cap'n Potts testily.

Rico sent Orinoco for the flannel, and meanwhile got the jolly-boat unshipped. By the time Orinoco returned, everything was ready; the boat was launched, Bosun was at the oars. A box of biscuits and a dozen of soda was provided, and Simon Sugar stood coughing by the taffrail. Rico let Cap'n Potts himself apply the flannel, as soon as Simon had removed the map; which he gave into the Captain's hands with a tear.

'Here you are, Cap'n,' he said, 'and thanks for all. Dear knows if we shall ever meet again.'

Then he was lowered carefully into the jolly-boat, and Bosun bent to his oars like one in a dream. As they pulled off, Cap'n Potts leaned over the rail and called through his megaphone, 'Bosun, what's your other name?'

'Alfred,' answered the Bosun.

'I somehow thought it might be,' said Cap'n Potts. Then he delivered Simon Sugar's map into the hands of Rico da Costa. There was a shout and a rush forward from the Pirates; but, 'No, you don't,' grins Rico. 'This is *my* pigeon. Nobody sets eyes on this map but me. You'll sail under my orders.'

'You ain't goin' to keep the Treasure to yourself, Rico?' inquired Orinoco, with a nasty look.

'Didn't you hear Simon Sugar say it'd do for the fifty of us?' asked Rico da Costa. 'What d'ye take me for? No, boys, it's share and share alike. But we've got to get there first.'

'And what about these?' asked Orinoco, waving his hand at the crew of the *Rockinghorse*. 'Shall we make 'em walk the plank?'

'That wouldn't be playing fair by Sugar,' said Rico. 'As I understand it there was a sort of understanding that their lives should be spared. So we'll take 'em along, and when they've helped us to load the Treasure up, we'll just maroon 'em and leave 'em to their fate.'

Then Rico da Costa divided us up, with some of the *Rockinghorse* crew and some of the *Marrowbone* Pirates aboard each ship; and he commanded the *Marrowbone* and left Orinoco in command of the *Rockinghorse*. I was in our ship with Cap'n Potts, and I could hardly bear to see that greasy pirate cock of our walk. I said as much to the Cap'n but he replied: 'Jim there's points about this I don't yet grasp. When Sugar parted from me he whispered "Just you keep hold of this, and trot it out when required. The *Marrowbone* was once the *Mary-le-bone*. I knew her again as soon as I set eyes on her."

So I'm not fretting Jim.'

I didn't see myself how Rico's chang-ing the name of a ship he'd captured

was going to help us; but as long as Cap'n Potts kept his pecker up I could keep up mine. We hadn't a ghost of a notion where we were bound for, but it took us a week to get there; because Rico da Costa would only sail by night, so that none of us should see the way we were going. And about dawn after the seventh night we fetched up on a rocky beach, and Rico da Costa said, 'Well, here we are!'

As far as we could see, that island kept itself inside a ring of rocks; over the tops of them we saw the green heads of palm trees, so we knew there must be vegetation inside. What did strike us was that we had never seen rocks anywhere with such a high polish on them; you could almost see your face in them. Another thing that struck us was the neatness of the beach itself; there wasn't a scrap of seaweed or litter of any sort to be seen; the pebbles, where there were pebbles, lay as even as setts in a road, and the sand, where there was sand, was as smooth as a carpet.

However, these were not things to occupy the minds of men set on finding an enormous Treasure. When we had disembarked, the Pirates came crowding round Rico da Costa crying, 'The map, Rico! Show us the map! Where does it say the Treasure is to be found?'

Rico saw that he must let them into the game a bit, so he took out the

map and said, unwillingly, 'It says the Treasure is mostly in the middle of the island, but works outward in every direction.'

'Hurrah!' cried Orinoco. 'Then it doesn't matter which way we go in! We're sure to trip over some of it on the way, till we reach the main hoard. Come along, lads!' And he started across the sands to an opening in the rocks, followed by half-a-hundred shouting Pirates.

They hadn't gone three yards, when a loud shrewish voice cried, 'Get off! Get off! Making footmarks all over my new-swept sand!'

Over the top of the rocks appeared the half of a woman, red in the face with anger. She was the most enormous figure of a woman you ever set eyes on, her arms were as thick as hams, and her huge hands brandished a broom that would crack a man's head.

'Get off!' she cried again.

The Pirates were so startled that they got off the sand at once, jumping sideways on to the rocks and pebbles. And then the woman shouted 'Get off those pebbles! Get off those rocks *at once*. Scratching my nice polish with your great ugly boots! Ugh! Look how you've messed the pebbles up. Put them back, every one of them, *do you hear*? Put them back this instant, just as they were!'

All the Pirates stooped immediately,

and tried to replace the pebbles as they had found them. We of the *Rockinghorse* had stayed beside the ship; and we stood looking on, wondering what would come next.

What did come next was the woman herself. She pushed herself through the widest gap in the rocks, and that was none too wide for her; and she bore down on Rico da Costa shouting, 'Take that pipe out of your mouth! Take it out, I say! D'you think I'm going to have tobacco-ash all over my island? Slave, slave, slave from morning to night, and that's all the thanks I get for it! A woman's work is never done!' she cried, and flourished her broom over Rico's head, much as he had

flourished his cutlass over Simon's.

When he could get his breath he began to say, 'Look here, Marm! I never asked you to slave for me. I don't know who you are!'

'And I don't know who *you* are,' retorted the big woman tartly. 'But since you *are* here, pushing your way in at spring-cleaning time, you'll just turn to and help.'

'I'm sure,' said Rico, 'we don't mind lending a hand to oblige a lady, do we, lads? But whatever do you find to do in the way of spring-cleaning on a desert island, ma'am?'

'Just like a man!' the woman snapped again. 'Nothing to do, you say? With the sea messing up the beach twice in every twenty-four hours; and the wind blowing the coconuts down, and the coconuts themselves all matted, and scratches on the rocks to get out, and the tree trunks needing varnishing, and what not! Nothing to do, indeed! Why, there's more to do here even than there was at home in Bristol City, where I wore myself to a bone keeping the place fit for Simon Sugar to live in.'

'For WHO?' cried Rico da Costa.

'Simon Sugar. *Now* what's wrong with you?'

'Who are you?' asked Rico da Costa, in trembling tones.

'Sarah Sugar, that's who I am.'

'And Simon Sugar is ——'

'My husband, of course. Well do I

remember our wedding day. "You've got a treasure in Sarah," my mother said to Simon. "If ever man married a treasure, you have today." And that's what I tried to be. I kept his house like a pin. I cleaned and scoured and scrubbed from morning to night. And was he grateful? No!'

'When did you see him last?' asked Rico da Costa; and if ever a Pirate spoke with his heart in his boots, Rico was that Pirate.

'Ten years ago,' said Sarah. 'He was sailing from Bristol City in the good ship *Mary-le-Bone*.'

'The *Mary-le-Bone*,' said Rico da Costa.

'The *Mary-le-Bone*,' said Sarah Sugar.

'It was spring-cleaning time, and some of the men, he told me, were staying at home to see their wives through. 'Ho!' I said, 'just like that.'

'Why,' asked Rico da Costa, 'did you say "Ho! just like that"?'

'Because it was so like the men, and so like the women! You'd never catch me with *my* house not cleaned half-way through spring-cleaning time.'

'Well,' I said to Simon, 'if you're short-handed on the *Mary-le-Bone*, I'll sail with you. I'm as good as fifty men any day when it comes to scrubbing. Simon said something about making it right with the Captain, but "I'll make it right with the Captain," I said, and so I did. We sailed the very next day for Lima.'

'For Lima,' said Rico da Costa.

'For Lima,' said Sarah Sugar. 'And you never saw such a mask of dirt on any ship in your life as I saw on the *Mary-le-Bone* when I got aboard. My word! I set them working! Before we got to Lima I had the ship as clean as a new pin. But we never did get to Lima.'

'How was that?' asked Rico.

'Why, one fine day we sighted this very island; and the Captain of the *Mary-le-Bone* said "There's Lima!" and I believed him. Then he turned very politely to me and asked, "Wouldn't you like to be the first ashore, Marm?" I'd small opinion of the Captain, but

it went up a point at that; and I said
I wouldn't mind. Next thing I knew,
Simon and I and the Bosun were
bundled into the jolly-boat, and rowed

to this very beach. "Out you hop!" said
the Bosun which, with Simon's help,
I did; and as soon as we'd landed the
Bosun turned the jolly-boat round and
rowed back to the *Mary-le-Bone*; and

then the *Mary-le-Bone* sailed away. Now, why did they do that?'

'Ask me another,' groaned Rico da Costa wearily.

'Well never mind,' said Sarah Sugar. 'I didn't. There was plenty to do on the island, as I soon found. It looked as though nobody'd ever tackled it since Creation; so I set to, and made Simon set to with me. It was almost more than one pair of hands could manage. Then *he* disappeared.'

'How?' asked Rico da Costa.

'I've never found out. Perhaps it was a tarantula.'

'You have tarantulas?' said Rico da Costa.

'Thick as cockroaches. Nasty teasing

critters. But I don't stand any of their nonsense. They fly when they see me coming!' Sarah Sugar flourished her broom again, and I fancy the thought in all our minds was thankfulness that we were not tarantulas seeing her coming.

'Well, that's the story,' said Sarah Sugar.

'Not all of it, surely, Marm,' said Rico da Costa. 'Haven't you left out the Treasure?'

'What Treasure?' asked Sarah Sugar.

'The Treasure on this island,' pleaded

Rico da Costa. 'The enormous Treasure that one man couldn't bear. The Treasure that would do for fifty men for life. The Treasure that is mainly in the middle of the island, and works outwards. Simon Sugar's Treasure, Marm! You've omitted to mention it.'

'I've omitted nothing,' snapped Sarah Sugar, 'and if there'd been any Treasure messing up my island I'd have found it long ago. Now then you men! I've no use for idle hands. Just come along and I'll show you where to begin!'

'Excuse me, Mrs. Sugar,' said Cap'n Potts. It was his first remark to her, and to tell you the truth she had been so surrounded with Pirates that she

hadn't seemed to notice us. But now she came sweeping through their ranks and looked us up and down. 'And who may *you* be?' she asked.

'Cap'n Potts, commanding the good ship *Rockinghorse*,' said he, saluting. 'And there she is.'

Sarah Sugar turned a critical eye on the *Rockinghorse*. She raked it fore and aft looking for dirt; and could she find a speck? No, she could not. 'A very tidy ship!' she admitted grudgingly.

'Can you say the same of that?' asked Cap'n Potts; and he pointed to the good ship *Marrowbone*.

Sarah Sugar let out a piercing shriek. 'As I'm alive,' cried she, 'it's the *Mary-le-Bone*!'

'It *was* the *Mary-le-Bone* till took by Pirates,' said Cap'n Potts. 'And then its name was changed, for deception's sake.'

'If you changed its name a dozen times you'd never deceive me,' said Sarah Sugar. 'I've scoured and polished that ship from top to toe. And look at it now! Worse than when I came aboard her with Simon. Who's responsible?' She rounded on Rico da Costa, who cowered before her. '*You*? Then all I've got to say to you is this: that ship's a disgrace to the Piracy!' She turned up her sleeves.

'Don't hit me!' cried Rico da Costa.

'Hit you!' she said witheringly. 'I wouldn't touch you with a marling-

spike—not till you've had a bath. Now then, all aboard!'

'What for?' asked Rico.

'To clean the *Mary-le-Bone*, of course,' said Sarah; 'a month's charring, as I see it.'

'And what about the *Rockinghorse*, Missus?' asked Cap'n Potts.

'The *Rockinghorse*?' She looked it over again. 'There's nothing to do for *that*. You can take yourselves and your ship off my island. Now then, pack off with you!'

We didn't need telling twice; and while Sarah Sugar bustled the Pirates aboard their dirty craft, the crew of the *Rockinghorse* manned her once again, and prepared to set sail. Only just as we veered about, Cap'n Potts called through his megaphone from the bridge: 'Mrs. Sugar!'

'What is it *now*?' she asked from the bridge of the *Marrowbone*.

'What was the name of the Bosun who landed you and Simon on this island?' asked Cap'n Potts.

'Alfie,' said she.

'I somehow thought it might be,' said Cap'n Potts. And we sailed away, leaving the Pirates up to their elbows in soap-suds.

We landed three days later in Lima, where all the Limen were waiting for us on the shore, with sacks of rubies. The Head Liman ran to meet us with open arms.

'We thought you were never coming!' he cried joyfully. We're so sick of lime-juice-cordial neat that it's all I can do to stop the folk from drinking the water again. We've got one case of pythonitis as it is. Have you brought the soda-water?'

'I have,' said Cap'n Potts, 'it's in the

hold.' In a jiffy we had it out, the Head Liman weighed it fairly and gave us its weight in rubies. After this he invited us all to an evening celebration, which Cap'n Potts accepted for everybody; and then he asked about the pythonitis case.

'He's not as bad as he might be,' said the Head Liman, 'for he hasn't scratched once, and the bumps are past the danger-zone.' He took us along to the wharf, and there we saw Simon Sugar and our Bosun. Bosun was sitting on Simon Sugar's hands; and Simon was looking out to sea, where a ship lay at anchor, with the jolly-boat just putting out. I must say Simon looked another man. The bumps had filled

him out, in a manner of speaking, and he had lost his cough.

'How's that?' asked Cap'n Potts, after the greetings and mutual rejoicings were over.

'You can't have pythonitis and a cough,' said Simon Sugar; 'according to the doctors' books they don't agree. I really owe my life to Alfred here; to stop me scratching, he's been sitting on my hands for three days, saying never a word.'

'He has a contemplative nature,' said Cap'n Potts, stroking Alfred's head. 'And now I suppose you're ready to go back.'

'Alfred will go back with you, but not me,' said Simon Sugar.

'I've booked a berth on the good ship *Demerara* over there. She sails for Bristol City in half an hour, and there's the Bosun coming to fetch me now.'

'Before you go,' said Cap'n Potts, 'I'd like to know two things. Why did you bother to make a map of that island, latitude and longitude an' all?'

'Because if I hadn't,' said Simon Sugar, 'I might have mistook the latitude and longitude.'

'I see,' said Cap'n Potts. 'The second thing is: why did you tell me you weren't a lawful married man?'

'I'm not,' said Simon Sugar. 'I'm a bigamist.' married x2 illegally

'I see,' said Cap'n Potts again; and then the Bosun of the good ship

Demerara fetched alongside, and Alfred got off Simon Sugar's hands, and handed Simon Sugar into his care. The Bosuns gave each other a thoughtful look, and parted. As the jolly-boat rowed back to the *Demerara*, Cap'n Potts called through his megaphone: 'Bosun! What's your name?'

'Alf!' yelled the Bosun.

'You know, Jim,' said Cap'n Potts, as we strolled into the city, 'I somehow thought it might be.'

That night the crew of the *Rockinghorse* joined the Limen in a great celebration of lime-juice-cordial and soda, than which there are few prettier tipples.

'They say, Cap'n,' said the Head

Liman, tossing off his third pint, 'that a good woman's worth is above the rubies—but I say, give me soda-water.'

'Quite so,' said Cap'n Potts.

'Is that all?' asked Quentin da Costa with round eyes.

'Of that one,' said Jim.

'I say! what happened to my great-grandfather?'

'Stayed on the island along o' Sarah Sugar.'

'I say! then how did I ——'

'Time you children went home to your dinner,' said Jim; and began to knock out his pipe.